The Mermaids and Yellow Jack. A NorFolktale

Written by **Lisa Suhay**

Illustrations by **Joan O'Brien**

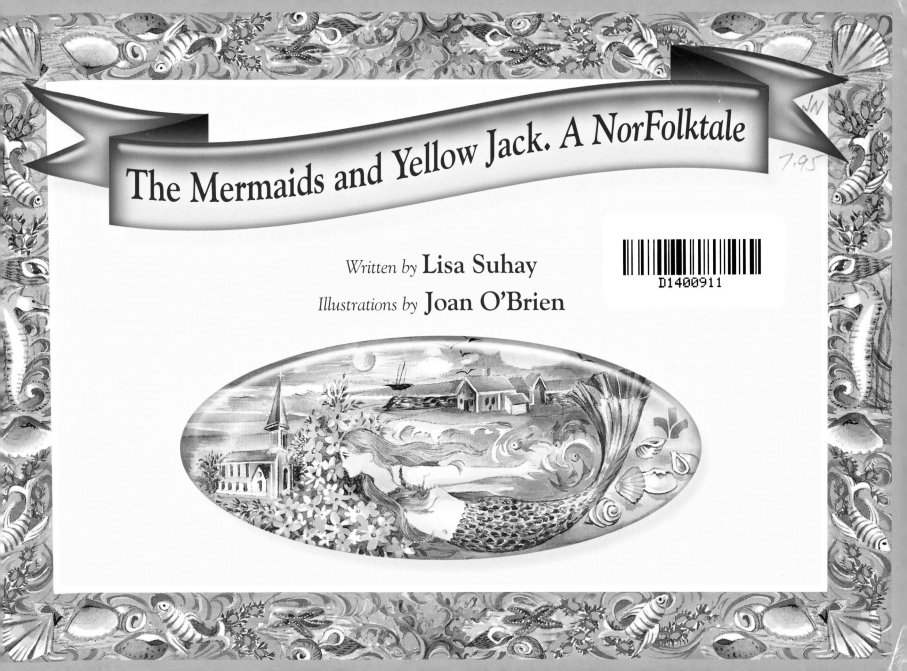

D1400911

In celebration of our anniversary, this book honors all those who, throughout our 150 years, have been a part of the DePaul family; in sickness and in health, as patients, care givers, staff, supporters, believers and dreamers.

— Bon Secours DePaul Medical Center, Norfolk, Virginia

For those who know a cool hand on a forehead and a friendly voice heal more than the body. Especially those at Bon Secours DePaul who delivered Quinten Coltrane Suhay. To Zoltan, Ian, Avery and Quin. Artist Georgia Mason "Mermaid Mamma" who created the nursemaid sculpture. Special thanks to Julie Paulina who summoned this mermaid.

— Lisa Suhay

Look for the Bon Secours fleur-de-lis hidden in the illustrations!

Cover and Book Design
Peri Poloni-Gabriel, Knockout Design, www.knockoutbooks.com

Printed in Singapore

All around the City of Norfolk, Virginia, people see beds of yellow flowers. They say there is a very important story behind them. They don't know how right they are!

One hundred and fifty years ago, in the waters of France, there lived a mermaid named Cara.

Cara and her friends were nursemaids in King Neptune's Jardin de Bon Secours (which means "Garden of Good Help" in French). They studied the healing powers of sea plants and learned the soothing songs of the Sirens.

It was a hot day in the year 1855 when Cara heard a clear ringing chime, like a glass bell. She swam toward the sound. It got louder and louder, until she had crossed the whole ocean and arrived at a little pier in Norfolk, Virginia, U.S.A.

A girl was sitting on the pier, crying so hard her salty tears fell into the water like rain.

It was the magic of those tears that called the mermaid. It is said nursemermaids can be called from a million miles away by a single tear, shed by a child in need.

"What makes you cry out an ocean?" the mermaid asked.

"It's a terrible sickness in the town—Yellow Fever," the girl sobbed. Her name was Aggie (named after her Aunt Agatha). "My Papa's a doctor. Nearly all my friends and neighbors are sick."

ara knew the sailors called this sickness "Yellow Jack." It was carried by ships from port to port.

King Neptune made up rhymes to help his nursemaids remember different sicknesses and cures.

What was the rhyme?

"Old pirate Yellow Jack
In warm weather will attack.
If fever spreads to the land,
Cool their heads
Hold their hands.
When rain turns to snow
Then will Yellow Fever go."

There was no cure, only comfort.

The mermaid came ashore to help. The second her hand touched dry land her tail transformed into legs and her shells and beads became a nurse's uniform.

"Oh my!" Cried Aggie. "If you can do magic like that you can make everyone well by magic too!"

The mermaid sighed, "There is no magic cure to human sickness. But I will do all I can to ease the suffering."

Cara reached into her pocket and pulled out a teeny little striped fish. "Candystripe, I need you to tell my friends they are needed to fight Yellow Jack!"

Candystripe leapt into the water and was gone.

Aggie led Cara to the homes of the sick. The mermaid placed her sea-cold hands on their fevered heads and sang to ease their suffering.

Eight more mermaids arrived with pouches of cold sea plants. They too cooled the heads and hearts of the sick.

The Yellow Fever raged on and on for 90-days until at last the cold weather came.

Just as King Neptune's rhyme foretold, rain turned to snow and the fevers *did* go. Yellow Jack was gone.

Since they were no longer needed, the mermaids decided to return to the sea. Nine nursemaids and Aggie stood on the freezing cold pier. The nursemaids joined hands and in one great leap — plunged into the river — becoming mermaids once more.

Unfortunately, Aggie's father saw the nursemaids SPLASH into the water!

The good doctor raised the alarm. Many came to search the icy waters. Since they never saw them come back to the surface, all believed they had drowned. Aggie tried to explain, "They're mermaids! They love cold water!"

Nobody believed her.

In the spring the city planted yellow flowers in memory of the Yellow Fever days. Because little Aggie insisted, the mermaid became the city symbol.

One hundred and fifty years after the mermaids left Aggie's dock, the hospital created a mermaid sculpture in memory of the nursemaids, to remind us all how charity did indeed come from across the sea.

Hundreds of mermaids from far and near attended the unveiling. But that's another story!

Photo by D. Kevin Elliott

Author's Note:

In creating this NorFolktale I have drawn from the remarkable histories of two sets of women — the Daughters of Charity and the Sisters of Bon Secours — whose legacies are entwined and embodied in the Bon Secours DePaul Medical Center we know today.

Birth of a Hospital

It was **June 1855** when the devastating yellow fever epidemic swept through Norfolk and Portsmouth — 6,000 people were stricken; 2,000 died.

The illness came into Tidewater from the Danish West Indies aboard the steamer *Ben Franklin*.

That tragedy and the heroism of eight sisters (nuns) of the order called **Daughters of Charity** laid the groundwork for the beginning of DePaul Medical Center.

As the disease spread these selfless women went from house to house caring for the ill. There was no cure for yellow fever, dubbed "Yellow Jack" by sailors. Only time and the alteration of weather to freezing temperatures ended the suffering of the stricken cities.

Ann Plume Behan Herron opened her home to the needy victims of the yellow fever epidemic. When the benefactor herself fell victim to the fever and died in 1856 her mansion was donated to the Daughters of Charity and became St. Vincent's hospital – the first in the area.

In 1899, St. Vincent's (after St. Vincent DePaul) burned down. The hospital was rebuilt in 1901 but soon outgrew it's capacity and in 1944 the medical center was relocated to its current location and renamed DePaul Hospital.

The DePaul Health Foundation was established in 1986 under the Daughters of Charity of DePaul Medical Center to manage the charitable donations made to the Medical Center.

The DePaul Medical Center was transferred from the **Daughters of Charity** to the **Sisters of Bon Secours** in 1996.

Proceeds will benefit the ongoing enhancements of patient care services at Bon Secours DePaul Medical Center.

Gifts to the Foundation go directly to strengthen programs, add new services, acquire cutting edge technology, or build new facilities. The goal of all projects and programs is to improve the health of our community's citizens. As a non profit organization, all gifts to the DePaul Health Foundation have a direct impact on the communities we serve, improving the health and well being of the thousands of patients and families we touch each year.

150th Anniversary
Celebrating 150 Years of Growing with the Community
1856 - 2006

BON SECOURS DEPAUL MEDICAL CENTER
Bon Secours Hampton Roads Health System

Photo by D. Kevin Elliott

The Sisters of Bon Secours

In Paris in 1824, amidst the devastation following the French Revolution, a group of 12 women, came together to form the congregation of the Sisters of Bon Secours, French for "good help". The sisters (nuns) left behind the security of their cloister to nurse the sick and dying in their homes.

In 1881, the congregation was invited to the Archdiocese of Baltimore and crossed the Atlantic to establish a health care ministry in Baltimore, Maryland. By 1909, convents were established in Washington, D.C. and in Detroit, Michigan.

The Sisters of Bon Secours provided the world's first recorded formal home health care service as well as the first day care facility in Baltimore in 1907 to help working mothers whose only alternative was to place their children in orphanages. St. Edmond's Home for Crippled Children, established in 1916, was the first Catholic home for the physically challenged.

The Sisters have a long tradition of willingness to take risks in pursuit of innovation, growth and extension of mission.

The Sisters of Bon Secours established their first hospital in Baltimore in 1919 and opened their second, in Grosse Pointe, Michigan, in 1945. By 1980, the Sisters had established and/or managed several Catholic hospitals, long-term care facilities and other health care services.

Illustrator:

Joan O'Brien is a resident of New York City. She was the recipient of a Fulbright scholarship to the Sorbonne University in Paris, Angers and Aubusson, France. Her fine arts background was first applied to printed and woven textiles, apparel and home furnishings. Her watercolor paintings have been exhibited in the Gallery at Madison 90 in New York City, Piccolo Mondo Gallery, Palm Beach and Capricorn Gallery in Washington, D.C. Ms. O'Brien is also known for a series of children's activity and coloring books for Dover Publishing. She is an Artist Resident Member of the Society of Illustrators in New York City. Contact the illustrator at jbobriendesigns@aol.com

Author:

Lisa Suhay is a resident of Norfolk, Virginia. She is a journalist and the mother of four boys. Mrs. Suhay worked with the City of Norfolk to create the Heart & Art Mermaid Story Trails, sponsored by Bon Secours DePaul Hospital System and The Virginian-Pilot Newspaper.

Other books by Lisa Suhay: *There Goes a Mermaid! A NorFolktale,* (The Virginian-Pilot Newspaper); *Tell Me a Story & Tell Me Another Story* (Paraclete Press); *Dream Catchers* (Marsh Media); *Haddy the Doorstopasaurus* (Franklin Mason Press) and *Our Fantasy Island* (Fantasy Island Amusement Park).